Alice
IN
Wonderland

LEWIS CARROLL

hinkler

hinkler

Published by Hinkler Books Pty Ltd
45–55 Fairchild Street
Heatherton Victoria 3202 Australia
www.hinkler.com.au

© Hinkler Books Pty Ltd 2003, 2017

Editor: Heather Hammonds
Cover Illustration: Terry Riley
Illustrations: Andrew Hopgood

ISBN: 978 1 4889 3156 7

Printed and bound in the USA

The Author
Lewis Carroll (1832–1898)

One hot summer day at Oxford in England, the Reverend Charles Dodgson, later known as writer Lewis Carroll, took three of his friend's young daughters for a picnic on the river.

As he rowed along, he told them delightful tales about a girl called Alice, and the nonsensical world of Wonderland. After the picnic he wrote the stories down, and was eventually persuaded to publish them under the title, *Alice's Adventures in Wonderland.*

Dodgson was born in Cheshire, England, the son of a churchman. He became a lecturer in mathematics at Oxford University and, later, a church deacon. However, he never took up a post as a priest due to a severe stammer.

His later books included *Through the Looking-Glass* and *The Hunting of the Snark,* published under the name of Lewis Carroll. He also published several books on mathematics, under his own name.

Contents

Chapter 1
The White Rabbit

Oh what a hot day it was! And what a most curious day it would turn out to be for young Alice. She and her sister had just finished a picnic by the pond in the meadow. They were sitting in the shade of a great oak tree.

Alice suddenly felt very sleepy. She yawned and wondered what to do next. She looked over to a grassy bank by the hedge. It was covered in daisies.

"I wonder," she thought, lazily, "if the pleasure of making a daisy chain is worth all the effort of getting up and picking the daisies?"

That was the moment she saw a White Rabbit with pink eyes, hurrying by the hedge. It was wearing a colourful waistcoat and it ran right past her.

For some reason, Alice didn't think that was odd at all. She didn't even think it a little strange when she heard the rabbit talking to itself.

"Oh dear! Oh dear!" said the White Rabbit. "I shall be too late. Oh dear! Oh dear!"

The Rabbit took a watch from its waistcoat pocket, looked at the time and then hurried on.

Alice was now very curious, and got to her feet. She followed the Rabbit and was just in time to see it pop down a rabbit hole, under the hedge. Without any hesitation, Alice followed it. She didn't give a thought to how she might get out again.

The rabbit hole took Alice into a long, dark tunnel. It seemed to go on for ages, before suddenly dropping away into what seemed to be a very deep well.

Now she was falling, and unable to stop herself. Either the well was very deep or she was falling very slowly, for as she fell, there was plenty of time to look about.

The sides of the well were covered with cupboards and bookshelves. Here and there Alice saw maps and hanging pictures. She reached out as she fell and took down a jar from one of the cupboards. It was labelled: *Orange marmalade.* She opened it but, to her disappointment, it was empty.

Alice continued falling. "Well, well," she

The rabbit ran right past her.

said. "After such a fall as this, I shall think nothing of tumbling downstairs again."

Down, down, down, she went. Would the fall never come to an end?

"How many miles have I fallen now?" she wondered. "I must be getting close to the centre of the earth. Let me see. That would be four thousand miles down, wouldn't it?"

Alice imagined she might fall right through the earth, come out the other side and find people walking on their heads.

Now she was falling.

Down, down, down. There was nothing else to do, so Alice continued talking to herself. "Dinah will miss me tonight, I should think."

Dinah was Alice's cat.

"I wish she was with me now," continued Alice. "There don't seem to be any mice here, but Dinah might catch a bat. And bats are a bit like mice. But do cats eat bats?"

Alice seemed to be dreaming. At first she was asking, "Do cats eat bats?" and then, "Do bats eat cats?"

Suddenly her fall came to an end. Thump!

Chapter 2
The Golden Key

Alice landed on a thick pile of sticks and dry leaves. She wasn't hurt and immediately jumped to her feet. She saw another tunnel ahead of her – and there was the White Rabbit scurrying along it.

Alice scampered after it.

The rabbit was still talking to itself. "Oh my ears and whiskers," it said, "how late it's getting."

Now Alice was close behind the animal. Not for long, though. The White Rabbit quickly turned a corner and vanished.

Alice reached the corner and found herself in a long, low hall. It was lit by a row of lamps hanging from the roof. The White Rabbit was nowhere to be seen.

There were lots of doors around the hall, but Alice found they were all locked. She was just wondering how she would ever get out of the hall when she spotted a little glass table

Alice found herself in a long, low hall.

in the middle of the room. Lying on the table was a tiny golden key!

Alice was sure the key would open one of the doors. She tried every one, but it was too small and didn't fit any of them.

Alice was about to give up, when her shoulder accidentally brushed aside a small curtain. Hidden behind it was a tiny door, no more than fifteen inches high.

She tried the golden key in the lock and, to her delight, it fitted! She opened the door. It led into a small passage, not much larger than a rat hole.

Alice knelt down and looked through the passage. She saw the loveliest garden she had ever seen. How she longed to escape from the hall and wander among the beds full of wonderful flowers. Better still, how she yearned to dance in the cool fountains she saw!

But the doorway was so small that she could not get her head through.

"And even if I could get my head through," thought poor Alice, "it would be very little use without my shoulders."

She turned and looked back at the table, on which she had found the key. She was amazed to see that a small bottle now stood on the table.

Looking through the passage.

It hadn't been there before, she was sure! And around the neck of the bottle was a label.

Alice locked the small door again and went back to the table. Printed on the label of the bottle were two words: *Drink me!*

Alice was no fool. She wasn't going to drink a bottle just because a label said she should. "I'd better look closer," she thought, "and make sure it doesn't say *poison* somewhere."

However, the bottle was not marked *poison*. So she put the golden key down on the table, slowly picked up the bottle and put it to her lips. She started to drink.

She found it very tasty. It had the flavour of cherry tart, pineapple, custard, roast turkey, toffee and hot-buttered toast and beans.

She finished it off in one gulp.

"What a curious feeling," said Alice, putting the bottle down on the floor. "I feel as if I've shrunk!"

And indeed she had. She was now only ten inches high. "How wonderful," she thought, "now I can get through the door and into the garden."

But first she waited to see if she was going to shrink any more. She was a bit nervous about that. "Perhaps," thought Alice, "I'll shrink until there is nothing left of me. I might vanish, just like a candle burning away to nothing."

After a while, nothing happened and Alice didn't get any smaller. So she went back to the little door. She was about to open it when she remembered she had left the key on the table. She turned around and was about to walk back.

"The table!" she exclaimed. "It's now so big and I'm so small. I can't reach the key!"

She walked over and did her best to climb up one of the table legs. It was too slippery and she just ended up in a heap on the floor. Alice tried it several more times but it proved impossible. She looked up at the golden key. It was so near, and yet so far away.

Finally, she sat down on the floor and burst into tears.

Chapter 3
Nine Feet Tall!

Alice didn't cry for long. "Come on!" she told herself. "It's no use crying. Stop this minute!"

Just then, she caught sight of a small glass box lying under the table. Once more, she was sure it hadn't been there before. She opened the box and found one very small cake inside. On the top of the cake were two words, spelt out in currants: *Eat me!*

"I shall eat it," said Alice. "Perhaps it will make me bigger. Then I can reach the key. And if it makes me smaller than ever, I can probably creep under the little door and get into the garden anyway."

Alice ate a small piece.

"Which way am I going?" she asked herself, a hand on her head to see if she was growing up or down.

She was surprised to find that she remained the same size. To be sure, this is what generally happened when one ate cake. But Alice had come to expect unexpected things to happen in the strange world where she now found herself.

She found it quite boring that nothing strange had happened. So she set about finishing the cake. Then something *did* start to happen.

"Curiouser and curiouser," said Alice, quite forgetting how to speak good English and using words she would never find, even in the most curious of dictionaries. "I think I'm being stretched out, and becoming taller and taller."

Eat me!

She looked down at her feet. They seemed to be disappearing into the distance. "Goodbye, feet," she said. "I don't know who will put on your stockings and shoes for you now. I won't be able to. I shall be a great deal too high above you to reach. You must do the best you can. But I promise to send you a new pair of boots for a present each Christmas."

Alice laughed. How strange it was to be talking of sending a present to one's own feet. She imagined the address on the parcel label:

Alice's right foot,
By the floor,
Close to the left foot.

She started to giggle. "What nonsense I am talking! Ouch!"

Just then, her head struck the roof of the hall. Alice was now very thin but rather more than nine feet tall. She started to cry again.

"You ought to be ashamed of yourself!" she sobbed. "A big girl like you, weeping away like this. Stop this instant, I tell you!"

But she couldn't. Alice kept on crying until there was a large pool of tears surrounding her. It was nearly six inches deep and reached halfway down the hall.

"Curiouser and curiouser."

Suddenly, the White Rabbit reappeared. He was now splendidly dressed, carrying a pair of white gloves and a large fan in his hand.

"Oh, the Duchess will be so angry," he mumbled to himself. "I'm late and she will be so angry. She'll be savage because I have kept her waiting."

"If you please, sir," cried Alice. "Can you help me?"

The White Rabbit stopped and took one glance at Alice. Then he dropped his white gloves and fan, and scurried away as fast as he could.

Chapter 4
The Pool of Tears

Alice stopped crying at last, and picked up the White Rabbit's gloves and fan. The hall was so hot that she started fanning herself.

"Dear, dear!" she said. "How odd everything is today. And yesterday everything was quite normal and dull."

Alice wondered if she had suddenly changed in the night. "Let me think," she said, "was I the same when I got up this morning? Come to think of it, I can remember feeling a little different. Perhaps I am no longer Alice at all."

Alice scratched her head. "But if I'm not Alice any more, then who in the world am I? That's the great puzzle!"

She thought about all the children she knew and wondered if she had been changed into one of them. "I'm sure I haven't become my friend Jenny," thought Alice. "She has ringlets in her hair and I don't. And I always knew more than little Sally. She's she, and I'm I."

Alice tried to remember all the things she knew before she went into the rabbit hole. "Let me see," she said, "I'll try adding some numbers together . . . two plus two make five . . . two plus four make seven . . . oh dear."

Alice had known how to add numbers before, but now she couldn't. "Never mind," she said, "I'll try geography."

Alice started listing some capital cities. "London is the capital of Paris. Paris is the capital of Rome and Rome is . . . oh dear."

She stopped again, as she knew she was talking nonsense. "Perhaps I've changed into Sally after all," she thought. "Sally always gets things wrong. But she was always good at remembering poetry. I'll try one of her favourites."

Alice recited a verse about a crocodile:

"How cheerfully he seems to grin,
How neatly spread his claws,
And welcomes little fishes in,
With gently smiling jaws!"

"Yes," she sighed. "They are the right words. I must have turned into Sally."

With that, poor Alice burst into tears again. If she had become Sally, then she would have

"How odd everything is today."

to live in Sally's little old house if she ever got back home.

"If I am Sally I'd rather stay down here than live in her house," she sobbed. "Yes, I will stay here."

Alice continued to cry, and the pool of tears was getting deeper all the time.

Then she noticed something strange. She looked down at her hands and saw that she had put on one of the White Rabbit's tiny, little gloves.

"How can I have done that?" she thought. "I must be shrinking again." She got up and went to measure herself by the glass table. Yes, she was now only two feet tall.

Alice was getting smaller at every moment and, of course, the pool of tears was getting deeper all the time. Fortunately, she discovered why she was shrinking. It was the fan she was using to keep cool. Immediately she stopped fanning herself and the shrinking stopped too.

"Phew!" she said. "That was a narrow escape. I nearly vanished into nothing."

She lost no time in deciding to get out of the big hall and find her way into the garden. She set off along the edge of the hall, carefully avoiding the pool of tears. But then she slipped

Alice continued to cry.

and tumbled in. Splash! Alice was soon up to her chin in salt water.

At first she thought she had fallen into the sea. "If that is the case," she said to herself, remembering past holidays with her parents, "then I can catch a train home from the seaside."

Alice soon recovered her senses. She had fallen into the great pool of her own tears.

Now she was in danger of drowning.

Chapter 5
Alice Swims for Her Life

"I wish I hadn't cried so much," said Alice as she swam about, trying to find her way out of the pool. "I'll be drowned in my own tears. That will be the oddest thing – but then, everything is strange and back-to-front today."

Just then, Alice heard something splashing about a little way off. At first she thought it must be a walrus, or even a hippopotamus. It was making such huge waves as it splashed around. Then she remembered how small she was. The waves just looked big.

Soon Alice saw what was really causing the waves. It was a small mouse that had fallen into the pool of tears. "Mouse!" she cried. "Do you know a way out of this pool? I am so tired I will soon drown."

The Mouse looked at Alice rather inquisitively, but didn't say a word. "Perhaps the Mouse doesn't understand English," thought Alice. "I expect it's a French mouse."

Alice had learned a little French in school. One of the few French words she knew was *chat*. It was the French word for *cat*. So she spoke to the Mouse again.

"Where is the chat?"

The Mouse gave a sudden leap out of the water and sat on a ledge, quivering with fright. It clearly understood both French and English!

"Oh, I beg your pardon!" cried Alice, afraid that she had hurt the Mouse's feelings. "I quite forgot that mice don't like cats."

"Not like cats!" cried the Mouse in a shrill voice. "Would you like cats if you were a mouse?"

"Well, perhaps not," replied Alice, glad to have her first conversation since entering the rabbit hole. "Please don't be angry. I have a cat myself. She's called Dinah and I'm sure you'd like her. She's a very gentle creature."

Alice swam over to the Mouse and rested on the ledge. She continued to talk about her cat and how nice she was.

"Please don't talk about cats any more, if you please," said the Mouse, still bristling with fear. "Our family always hated cats – nasty creatures with sharp claws."

Alice apologised again. "I won't say another

A small mouse had fallen in.

word about them. But I do know a nice dog that lives near our house. Let me tell you about him. He's a bright-eyed terrier with long curly brown hair. If you throw something he'll go and bring it back for you. He'll also sit and beg for his dinner."

That was too much for the Mouse. It dived into the water and started swimming away.

"Oh, sorry," she called out. "Do come back! I promise I won't mention cats or dogs again."

When the Mouse heard that, it turned around and swam back to the ledge.

"If you will listen to my story," it said, "you will understand why I hate cats and dogs. Follow me."

It was then that Alice noticed something else. Lots of birds had found her pool of tears and were enjoying a swim. She saw a duck and a dodo bird, a parrot, a young eagle and a magpie. There were also lots of other creatures that had fallen in. The pool had become quite crowded.

The Mouse swam off and Alice followed it. So did all the other creatures.

A little later they all reached the safety of a grassy bank. Alice was glad to be out of the pool of tears at last.

The pool had become quite crowded.

Everyone was dripping wet and bedraggled, and wanted to know how they could get dry again.

Alice found herself talking to the creatures as though she had known them all her life. She even had an argument with the Parrot, who insisted he should speak first because he was older. When she asked him how old he was, he refused to say.

"In that case," said Alice firmly, "I shall have my say first."

Alice was interrupted by the Mouse. It seemed to have some special authority among the creatures.

"Sit down, all of you and listen to me!" it said. "I'll soon make you all dry. Now stand in a circle around me."

They formed a circle around the Mouse and it began to say the strangest things. First, it listed all the kings of England. Then it named all the wives of King Henry the Eighth. Next came a list of all the rivers of England and Scotland, and the names of all the wildflowers in the meadows.

"I'm still wet," complained Alice, wondering how on earth the Mouse hoped to dry everyone by giving history and geography lessons.

"So am I," said the Duck.

"In that case," said the Dodo bird, "we must arrange a meeting to discuss the problem."

"Oh stop waffling!" cried the Eagle. "We don't need a meeting to decide how to get dry."

"Then," said the Dodo, "we'll have a Dodo Race instead. That will dry us."

"What's a Dodo Race?" asked the Parrot.

"The best way to show you is to have one," answered the Dodo. "Now line up behind me."

Chapter 6
The Tale of the Mouse's Tail

Alice and everyone else lined up, and the Dodo shouted, "Go! Follow me!"

They all raced after the Dodo. They raced and raced and raced. There seemed no end to the race. But after running for half an hour they stopped, because they were all dry again.

"The race is over!" declared the Dodo. "Everyone is dry."

"But who won the race?" asked the Duck.

"That's easy to answer," said the Dodo. "We all did because we are all dry. Now, there will be prizes for everyone."

"And who will give the prizes?" asked the Magpie.

"Why the girl of course," said the Dodo, pointing at Alice.

All the creatures crowded around Alice, asking for their prizes. Poor Alice had no idea what to give them. She put her hand in her pocket and found some sweets. She

Racing after the Dodo.

gave a sweet to everyone.

"Alice must have a present too," said the Dodo. "Alice, what else have you got in your pocket?"

She pulled out a thimble. The Dodo took it and then immediately presented it back to her. "This is your prize," it announced solemnly.

Alice thought the whole business of the race and the prizes quite mad. She felt like bursting out with laughter, but everyone there seemed to be so serious. She didn't even dare to giggle.

She accepted her own thimble with a solemn expression of gratitude. How everyone applauded!

"Curiouser and curiouser," thought Alice.

After Alice had returned the thimble to her pocket, she turned to the Mouse. "You promised to tell me your story," she said, "and explain why you hate cats and dogs."

The Mouse went very quiet. "Mine is a long and sad tale," it began.

"You certainly have a long tail," said Alice, looking down with wonder at the Mouse's tail. "But why do you call it sad?"

"If you're going to make fun of my tail with words," said the Mouse indignantly, "then I won't tell my story."

"Mine is a long and sad tale."

Alice said she was sorry. "Please tell me your story," she begged.

"Yes!" cried everyone else. "Please tell us your story."

So the Mouse began its story. But the strangest thing happened. Alice found her mind wandering all over the place. At one time it was in a courtroom with lots of little animals, arguing with a judge. She couldn't concentrate on what the Mouse was saying at all.

The Mouse quickly spotted that she wasn't paying attention to its story.

"You are not listening to me," it said angrily.

"Yes, I was," answered Alice, knowing full well she had not been listening.

"What was I just saying then?" it snapped.

"Er . . . Ah . . . Um . . ." said Alice, desperately trying to imagine what it had been saying. "The weather. You were talking about the weather."

"No!" it cried. "You have insulted me by not listening to my tale. I shall not stay. I'm leaving."

With that, it scurried off.

"Oh do come back and finish your story," cried Alice.

The others joined in. "Yes, please do," they called.

But the Mouse just shook its head impatiently and hurried away as fast as it could.

"I wish Dinah was here," said Alice, "She'd soon fetch the Mouse back."

"And who is Dinah, if I dare ask such a question?" inquired the Parrot.

"Dinah is my cat," replied Alice. "And she's very clever at catching mice. Birds too. I wish you could see how she catches birds. Why, she'd eat a bird as soon as look at it!"

Alice suddenly wished she hadn't said anything at all about Dinah. Birds were just as scared of cats as mice were.

All the birds became very agitated. Some of them hurried away at once. The Magpie started to wrap itself up in brown paper. "I really must be getting home now," it said.

A young canary called out in a trembling voice to its children. "Come away, my dears! It's high time you were all in bed."

One by one all the creatures, using one excuse or another, wandered away.

"Oh how I wish I had never mentioned Dinah," said Alice quietly to herself. "She's such a nice cat, but no one down here seems to like her."

Alice felt so lonely, and she began to cry again.

After a while, she heard a pattering of footsteps in the distance. She looked up eagerly, hoping that the Mouse had changed its mind and was returning to finish its story.

But it wasn't the Mouse. It was the White Rabbit.

Chapter 7
The White Rabbit's House

The White Rabbit had returned to find its gloves and fan. Suddenly, the creature saw Alice. "Run home this minute!" it said angrily, mistaking Alice for its housemaid. "Fetch me a pair of white gloves and a fan. Quick, now!"

To make sure Alice understood, the White Rabbit pointed in the direction she should go.

Alice had no idea why the Rabbit was angry with her. After all, she wasn't the one who had lost the gloves and fan. But she was so frightened that she ran off at once, in the direction the White Rabbit was pointing.

She soon came to a neat little house. On the door was a shiny brass plate engraved *W. Rabbit*. She went in without knocking, and climbed up the stairs to look for some gloves and a fan.

Alice found her way into a small room with a bed, a dressing table and one window. To her delight, she saw a fan and three pairs of white gloves on the table.

She picked up the fan and one of the pairs of gloves. She was about to leave when she spotted a little bottle by the mirror. This time there was no label on it saying something like: *Drink me!* But she knew that the bottle must contain some magical liquid.

"Whenever I eat or drink here, something happens," she thought, as she opened the bottle.

"Run home this minute!"

"So I'll just see what this bottle does. I hope it will make me grow larger again because I am really tired of being such a tiny little thing."

Alice put the bottle to her lips and drank. Whoosh! She was growing again!

The next moment her head was pressing hard against the ceiling, and she had to stoop down to save her neck from being broken.

Alice didn't want to grow another inch, so she quickly put down the bottle. "As it is," she said, "I'm already too big to get out of the door. I wish I hadn't drunk from that bottle."

Alas! It was too late now. Alice went on growing and growing. Her back stretched further and further and her legs grew longer and longer. Soon she had to kneel on the floor to fit herself into the room.

Alice had to hunch down while leaning on one elbow, with the other resting against the door. Still she grew. Now she put one arm out of the window and one foot up the chimney.

"This is the end," she said. "I can't grow any more. If I do, I will be squeezed to death."

Luckily, right at that moment, the effects of the drink wore off. She stopped growing at last – but she was now completely wedged into the room with no hope of getting out.

Whoosh! She was growing again!

"It was much nicer at home," Alice thought sadly, "when I wasn't growing larger or smaller every moment. I almost wish I'd never gone down that rabbit hole."

But she didn't really mean it.

"I'd like to discover what has happened to me," she decided. "When I used to read fairytales I always thought those strange things could never happen. And now here I am, right in the middle of my own fairytale! And I'd like to get to the end of it before I go home."

Alice's thoughts and imaginings were suddenly interrupted by the sound of the front door opening and the slamming shut.

Then she heard the pattering of little feet, scurrying up the stairs . . .

Chapter 8
Trapped!

"Where's that girl with my gloves and fan?" shouted an impatient voice. "Where are you? Have you got my gloves and fan yet? Do hurry up! I can't wait!"

Alice realised it was the White Rabbit coming to look for her. She started to shiver and shake with fright. She was so tightly trapped in the room that for her every shiver and shake, the house itself trembled. Of course, Alice had no need to be frightened. She was quite a thousand times larger than the White Rabbit now.

The Rabbit reached the door and tried to open it. It pushed and pulled, but it couldn't get in because of Alice's body. Alice tried to move herself, but she only managed to make the room shake, as if there was a small earthquake. She heard the White Rabbit squeak with fright.

"There's something in there that's blocking the door!" it cried.

It pushed and pulled, but it couldn't get in.

There was silence for a moment. Then the White Rabbit started thinking out aloud. "I know," it said, "I'll go outside and climb in by the window."

Alice heard the Rabbit run downstairs and out of the front door. Soon it was trying to scramble up the wall beneath her window.

Alice's arm was still hanging out of the window and she decided to try and help the Rabbit climb up. She could move her arm a tiny bit and as soon as she thought the Rabbit was within reach, she opened her hand wide and made a grab for it.

For a moment, Alice thought she had caught the Rabbit. But her hold wasn't strong enough and she felt the creature slip from her hand. She heard a little shriek and then a great thump, as the Rabbit hit the ground. The next thing she heard was a very angry voice – the Rabbit's.

"Pat! Pat! Come here this instant!" it cried. "Where are you, Pat? Have you fallen asleep again?"

Alice had no idea who Pat was.

"Sure, I'm not asleep," answered a voice Alice hadn't heard before. "I'm here digging apples in the vegetable garden."

Making a grab for the White Rabbit.

She guessed that Pat must be the gardener.

Once more Alice thought how curious this new world was. When did apples grow in the soil like potatoes? "Oh well," she thought, "I'm getting used to everything being back to front and upside down here."

The Rabbit started to rant and rave. "Digging apples indeed!" it cried. "Pat, you get here right away and help me!"

Alice heard the sound of footsteps approaching the window.

"To be sure, you're in a mess," said Pat.

"Never mind me for the moment," said the White Rabbit. "What do you see hanging out of the window?"

"Sure, it's an arm!" said Pat. "And it's got a hand on the end of it."

"An arm!" exclaimed the White Rabbit. "Of course, it's an arm. But whoever saw an arm so large? It fills the whole window."

"Sure it does, your honour, but it's still an arm for all that," said Pat.

Alice heard the Rabbit sigh. "Well, that arm has no right to be there," said the Rabbit. "Please take it away immediately!"

There was a long silence after this. Alice could only hear whispers now and then.

"I don't like this business at all," said Pat. "The arm might attack me."

"Do as I say!" said the Rabbit. "You're a coward!"

Alice was quite frightened now, in case Pat decided to chop her arm off. So she shouted and screamed and waved her arm about as fast as she could.

Then she heard someone say, "We must go for help!"

The sound of the Rabbit and Pat's footsteps gradually faded away into the distance.

"Now what?" wondered Alice.

Chapter 9
Bill in the Chimney

Some time later, Alice heard the sound of a group of creatures coming back. They all seemed to be talking and shouting at each other. As they arrived beneath the window, she could make out what some of them were saying.

"Eh, have you brought two ladders?" asked a voice.

"Nope!" said another. "I've got one. Bill's got the other."

"Well we can't get up to the window without both," said the first voice.

"Bill! Bill!" cried the second voice. "Bring your ladder over."

Alice heard someone else arrive beneath the window. "It must be Bill," she thought.

"Now Bill," said the first voice. "Tie these two ladders together and put them up to the window."

Alice heard lots of noises after that. She guessed Bill was doing his best to tie the ladders

"Bill! Bill! Bring your ladder over."

together. There were sounds of a struggle and lots of other people offering Bill advice.

"Do it this way!" "Do it that way!" "Turn the ladders the other way!" "Turn them over!" "Turn them up!" "Turn them down!" "Up she goes!"

Then Alice heard a sharp cry. "Mind the roof tiles, Bill!"

"Watch out!" shouted another voice.

"Oops!"

"Aaaggghhh!"

There was a great crash! Alice knew that the ladder – with Bill on it – must have fallen to the ground. Once more there was silence. Then a quiet voice said, "Bill! Bill! Are you okay?"

A little while after, Bill groaned that he was all right.

"Oh that's good," said the voice, "because it might be easier to try and get into the room by climbing down the chimney instead."

Alice thought it so unfair that poor old Bill had to do everything. "I wouldn't be in Bill's shoes for anything," she thought.

With that, she wiggled the toes of her foot. She found she could move her foot quite freely in the chimney.

This was useful because the next thing she knew was that Bill – whoever or whatever he was – had entered the chimney. Alice heard him scratching and scrambling about, close to her foot.

Now she was frightened again. What if Bill was a great rat with huge teeth? What if he started to nibble at her toes? Frightened, she kicked out with her foot. The power was just enough to eject Bill from the chimney.

If Alice had been able to look outside, she would have been surprised to see a small lizard shoot out of the chimney, as if he had a rocket beneath him.

"There goes Bill!" shouted the Rabbit.

"Catch him if you can," said another voice.

Bill fell to earth with a crash.

"What happened?" asked the Rabbit.

"Well, I hardly know," squeaked Bill, quite out of breath. "I'm a good deal too flustered to remember. But I think someone must have put a jack-in-the-box in the chimney. And up I goes, like a skyrocket!"

"And so you did, Bill" cried the others. "You flew into the sky."

"There's something very strange going on here," said the White Rabbit. "We cannot take any more risks with this strange arm hanging out of the window and something else quite

Shooting out of the chimney.

odd in the chimney. We must burn the house down!"

Alice hadn't called out one word during the whole episode. She had been too frightened to say anything.

But now they were going to burn the house down!

Chapter 10
Alice's Escape

"If you burn the house down, I'll set my cat Dinah on you," Alice called out, as loudly as she could.

She guessed there must have been some mice outside, because suddenly there was lots of squeaking, and the sound of creatures running about.

Then she heard them all discussing a new plan, saying a barrowful of something would do the job.

"A barrowful of what?" wondered Alice.

The next moment she heard a shower of pebbles rattling against the window. A few hit her on the face and stung her.

"You'd better not do that again!" she shouted down.

That produced another dead silence outside. Alice guessed they were thinking what to do next.

Alice looked at some of the pebbles they

had thrown up at the window. They were not pebbles at all, but tiny cakes. All at once, a bright idea came into her head. Everything she had eaten or drunk since climbing down the rabbit hole had made her either grow taller or shrink.

"Perhaps I'll eat a few of those little cakes," she thought. "I'll either get so big that I'll burst out of the top of the house, or get smaller so I can get out of this room."

So she ate some of them. Alice found them very tasty.

"You'd better not do that again!"

"I'm shrinking again!" she shouted in delight.

Inch by inch, Alice grew smaller. Soon, she freed her leg from the chimney. Not long after she was able to stand up again. She heard gasps from outside when she finally brought her arm back through the window. She sighed with relief and hurried downstairs, and out of the house.

Alice was very surprised at the big crowd outside. The White Rabbit was there. So were lots of other little creatures. And in the middle, lying down and looking rather wounded from his flight from the chimney was Bill, a rather sad-eyed green lizard.

Two guinea-pigs were holding his head up and trying to make him drink some sort of medicine.

When the creatures saw Alice, they immediately made a rush at her. Being so small again, she dare not stay. So she ran off as fast as she could and escaped into a nearby wood. She felt quite safe there.

"Now," she said, "what shall I do?"

She decided that the first thing was to get a little taller again. Alice looked around to see if there was anything to eat and spotted a mushroom growing nearby. It was about the same height as her.

A crowd of little creatures.

Alice walked around it. She looked underneath it. She looked all around it. Then she thought she might as well see what was on top of it.

She stretched herself up on tiptoe and peeped over the edge of the mushroom.

"My goodness!" she shrieked.

Chapter 11
Advice from a Caterpillar

Alice found herself staring straight into the eyes of a large blue caterpillar.

"And who are you?" it asked, in a lazy, sleepy sort of way.

"I . . . I hardly know just at this moment, sir," she answered as politely as she could. "At least, I know who I was when I got up this morning. I also knew who I was when I went for a picnic with my sister. But I think I may have changed several times since then."

"What do you mean by that?" asked the Caterpillar, sternly. "Explain yourself!"

"I can't explain myself, sir," answered Alice. "I can't because I'm not myself this afternoon, or whatever time of day it is. I'm just not myself, you see."

"I don't see at all," said the Caterpillar.

"I'm afraid I can't put it any more clearly," said Alice, "because I can't understand it. How can I explain myself when I have been

Staring into the eyes of a large blue caterpillar.

so many different sizes all in one day? It is very confusing."

"It isn't," said the Caterpillar.

"Then, perhaps, sir," said Alice rather more boldly, "you haven't experienced changing in size and shape yet."

"I won't either!" answered the Caterpillar.

"Yes, you will," said Alice. "Just wait until you turn from a caterpillar into a butterfly!"

"Oh, stuff and nonsense," said the Caterpillar. "Now tell me who you are!"

Alice was quite irritated to find that the conversation was now back where it had started. "I think," she said, "it would be best if you tell me who you are first."

"Why?" said the Caterpillar.

Alice couldn't think of a good reason why the Caterpillar should tell her first. He was so unpleasant that she became angry, and walked away without saying another word.

"Come back! Come back!" cried the Caterpillar. "I've got something important to say."

Alice turned and came back, hoping to hear something useful.

"Keep your temper, girl," said the Caterpillar. "Don't lose your temper just because you can't have everything your own way."

"Come back! Come back!"

"Is that all?" snapped Alice.

"No," said the Caterpillar.

Alice decided she might as well wait to see what the Caterpillar had to say. After all, she had nothing better to do. So she clambered onto the top of the mushroom and sat down.

"So you think you've changed, do you?" said the Caterpillar.

"I think so, sir," Alice answered. "I can't remember things as I used to. And I don't stay the same size from one minute to the next!"

"Can't remember what things?" asked the Caterpillar.

Alice thought for a moment, before speaking, "I can't remember verses I knew before," she said.

"Do you know the poem *You are old, Father William?*" asked the Caterpillar.

"I used to," replied Alice.

And so she began to try and recite it:

*"'You are old Father William,' the young
    man said,
'And your hair has become very white;
And yet you incessantly stand on your head-
Do you think, at your age, it is right?'*

'In my youth,' Father William replied to his son,

'I feared it might injure the brain;
But now that I'm perfectly sure I have none,
Why, I do it again and again.'

'You are old,' said the youth, 'as I mentioned
    before,
And have grown most uncommonly fat;
Yet you turned a back-somersault in at the door,
Pray, what is the reason for that?'

'In my youth,' said the sage, as he shook his
    grey locks,
'I kept all my limbs very supple
By the use of this ointment – one shilling the
    box –
Allow me to sell you a couple?'

'You are old,' said the youth, 'and your jaws
    are too weak
For anything tougher than suet;
Yet you finished the goose, with the bones and
    the beak –
Pray, how did you manage to do it?'

'In my youth,' said his father, 'I took it to law,
And argued each case with my wife;
And the muscular strength, which it gave to
    my jaw,
Has lasted the rest of my life.'

"You are old, Father William."

*'You are old,' said the youth, 'one would
  hardly suppose
That your eye was as steady as ever;
Yet you balanced an eel on the end of your
  nose –
What made you so awfully clever?'*

*'I have answered three questions, and that is
  enough,'
Said his father; 'Don't give yourself airs!
Do you think I can listen all day to such
  stuff?
Be off, or I'll kick you downstairs!' "*

"That's not the poem I remember," said the
Caterpillar. "It was wrong from beginning to
end."

"I know," said Alice. "I seem to have forgotten the proper words."

There was silence for a few moments before
the Caterpillar asked another question. "And
what size do you want to be?"

"A little bigger, though I don't really mind
what size I am," said Alice, "as long as I don't
keep changing all the time."

"Are you happy with your size now?" asked
the Caterpillar.

"Well, to tell you the truth I would like to be a little larger," she replied. "Being only three inches tall is a rather funny height to be, after all."

"I don't know why you should complain," replied the Caterpillar, drawing itself up to its full height.

How odd. The creature was exactly three inches tall as well.

"Three inches is a good height to be," it said.

"It is indeed, if you are used to being that height," said Alice. "But I am used to being taller."

"You will soon get used to being three inches tall," replied the Caterpillar.

With that, it got up and crawled down the mushroom. "Try eating this mushroom," it said. "One side will make you grow taller, and the other will make you shorter."

Then the Caterpillar crawled away and disappeared into the undergrowth.

Alice reached up and broke off two pieces of the mushroom, one from either side of it. She ate a little from the left-hand side of the mushroom and put the rest in her pocket.

She had hardly swallowed the mushroom when she started to grow at great speed!

Chapter 12
The Angry Pigeon

Oh dear, how Alice grew!

She looked down towards her shoulders. They were nowhere to be seen. And where were her feet? She could not see them either. All she could see was a huge length of neck, and nothing else.

Alice's neck now seemed to rise like a great stalk out of a sea of green leaves that lay far below her. "What can all that green stuff be?" she wondered. "And where have my shoulders gone to? Where are my hands and feet?"

As there was no hope of getting her hands up to her head, Alice tried to get her head down to some faraway place where her shoulders, hands and feet might be. She was delighted to find that her neck would bend in any direction as easily as a piece of elastic. She could move it rather like a snake might.

Alice had succeeded in moving her neck down in a graceful zigzag and was about to dive

Her neck would bend in any direction.

into the leaves, when she discovered something very strange. The things she imagined were green leaves were, in fact, treetops.

Suddenly, a pigeon came swooping out of one of the trees. It flew around Alice, flapping its wings in her face and crying, "Serpent!"

"I'm not a serpent!" exclaimed Alice. "Leave me alone!"

"Serpent, I say again," repeated the Pigeon. "And there's nothing that seems to frighten off you and your kind. You're forever stealing my eggs."

Alice was puzzled. She said she hadn't the least idea what the Pigeon was talking about.

"I've nested in the roots of the trees," said the Pigeon, "and I've nested in hedges and the banks beneath them. But those serpents! They get everywhere."

Poor Alice was, by this time, very confused.

"As if it wasn't enough trouble hatching my eggs," the Pigeon continued, "but now I must be on the look-out for serpents night and day! Why, I haven't had a wink of sleep for three weeks!"

"I'm sorry," said Alice, "I seem to have annoyed you."

"And just as I was thinking that I was free

"I'm not a serpent!"

of serpents," said the Pigeon, "what happens? Another one comes wriggling out of the sky."

"But I'm not a serpent!" cried Alice. "I'm a . . . I'm a . . ."

"Yes! Yes!" said the Pigeon. "What are you?"

"I . . . I'm a little girl!" Alice said at last.

"A likely story indeed," said the Pigeon, who clearly didn't believe a word of it. "I've seen a good many girls in my time, but never one with a neck like yours. No! No! You are a serpent and there's no use you denying it. I suppose you'll be telling me next that you've never stolen a bird's egg and eaten it."

"I've eaten plenty of eggs like any little girl," said Alice, "but I've never stolen a bird's egg like a serpent might."

"I don't believe it," said the Pigeon. "If little girls do eat eggs as you say, then it just means that little girls are just another sort of serpent. And I have caught you egg hunting. So there you are. It doesn't matter whether you are a little girl or a serpent."

"Well!" said Alice, angrily. "It matters a great deal to me and I'm not looking for any birds' eggs – especially not yours."

"Well, in that case, be gone with you!" said

the Pigeon, in a very sulky tone, before flying off to its nest.

Alice walked on, taking a nibble of both of the pieces of mushroom that she had saved.

In turn, she grew taller and then shorter, depending on whether she ate on the left or right piece of the mushroom. It took some very careful nibbling on both pieces before she at last returned to her normal size.

It had been so long since Alice had been her normal size that it felt very strange at first. But she soon got used to it and set about completing the next bit of her plan . . . to find a way into the beautiful garden she had seen.

So Alice wandered off, not really knowing where she was going. She found herself in a forest and soon after, she saw a tiny cottage through the trees. It was so small that the roof was only as high as Alice's ankles.

"Oh dear," she thought. "Now I'm back to my normal size, I shall certainly frighten anyone who lives in this little place."

So she nibbled on the left side of the piece of mushroom. Soon she had shrunk herself down until she was just nine inches tall again.

Chapter 13
The Fish and the Frog

Alice was approaching the little cottage when a footman in a very smart uniform came running out of the forest.

Now, Alice knew that a footman was a kind of servant who worked for a King or a Queen, or a wealthy Lord. She knew he had to be a footman because of his special uniform.

But she still couldn't escape the fact that despite his fine clothes and enormous curly wig, this footman was in fact a fish on two legs!

The Fish Footman knocked on the door of the cottage and waited. It was opened by another footman. He had a round face and large bulging eyes. Alice saw that beneath his richly embroidered clothes and curly wig, he was a frog.

The Frog Footman came out of the cottage and shut the door behind him. Alice grew very curious and crept a little further out of the wood, so she could listen to what they were saying.

The Fish Footman handed over a large and very important-looking envelope to the Frog Footman. The back of the envelope was sealed with the picture of a large royal crown.

"This is an invitation for the Duchess," said the Fish Footman, "to play a game of croquet with the Queen."

"The Duchess will be pleased," answered the Frog Footman, taking the letter.

The Fish Footman and the Frog Footman then bowed to each other, their two wigs becoming quite entangled.

Alice laughed out aloud as they struggled to free themselves. The Fish Footman turned around to see who had made the noise. He took one look at Alice, put his nose in the air and walked off.

The Frog Footman was about to do the same and walk back into the house, but Alice hurried over to ring the doorbell.

"It's no use ringing the bell," said the Frog Footman.

"Why?" asked Alice.

"Two reasons," he replied. "First, the door is shut and I am outside the house. So if you

They struggled to free themselves.

ring I'll still be outside and won't be able to open the door for you. And secondly, they are making such a noise in there that no one will hear you ring anyway."

And certainly there was an extraordinary noise coming from inside; a howling and sneezing sort of noise, occasionally interrupted by a great crash. Alice thought someone must be throwing kettles and saucepans around.

"If there is no point in my ringing the bell," said Alice, "how am I going to get in?"

"You could try knocking," answered the Frog Footman. "In fact, if you were inside you could knock and I could answer the door from here, and let you out of the house."

"But I want to go in," said Alice impatiently.

The next thing Alice knew was that the door had suddenly opened and out flew a large plate. It hit the Footman a glancing blow on the nose and then smashed to pieces on a nearby tree. The door then slammed shut again.

The Frog Footman took no notice at all, although he did scratch his nose once.

"So, *how* do I get in?" asked Alice, starting to get very angry.

"Are you to get in at all?" said the Footman. "That's the first question, you know."

"Do you always answer a question with another one?" cried Alice. "It's enough to drive a person crazy."

"Oh well," said the Footman. "I shall say nothing then. I shall just sit here in silence for the next three years."

"But what am I to do?" pleaded Alice.

"Do what you like," he answered. "Even if you go in, the Duchess won't want to talk to you. She won't have time for the likes of you."

Enough was enough. Alice ignored the Foot-

"It's no use ringing the bell."

man, opened the door for herself and walked in. The door led straight into a kitchen. It was full of smoke, from one end to the other.

Through the smoky haze, Alice saw three people. One was a cook, who was stirring a large pot of soup on the stove. And sitting on a three-legged stool in the middle of the room was a huge woman, nursing what appeared to be a baby with a shawl wrapped around its head.

The woman was wearing a very grand gown, and a very strange hat that looked a bit like an upside-down crown.

Alice guessed that this woman must be the Duchess.

Chapter 14
The Duchess

"There's too much pepper in the soup!" shouted the Duchess, nearly dropping the baby on the stone floor. "Atishoo!"

"I dropped the . . . atishoo! . . . pepper pot in the soup," said the Cook. "Atishoo!"

"Stupid woman!" shrieked the Duchess.

To Alice, the air seemed full of pepper.

"And who . . . atishoo! . . . are you?" asked the Duchess, seeing Alice at last.

"I'm Alice and I'm looking . . . atishoo! . . . for a beautiful garden," sneezed Alice.

Just then, she noticed a huge cat sitting by the stove. It was grinning. "Why is that cat grinning?" she asked.

"Because it's a Cheshire Cat," replied the Duchess. "That's why!"

"I have never heard of a Cheshire Cat," said Alice, "and I certainly didn't know they could grin. In fact, I didn't know that any cat could grin."

Too much pepper in the soup.

"All cats grin!" said the Duchess sharply. "Especially Cheshire Cats."

"Sorry, I didn't know," said Alice.

"That shows how little you know," snapped the Duchess, who seemed to be a very irritable person.

At that moment, the Cook picked up an armful of empty kettles, pots and pans, and started showering the Duchess with them. The Duchess took no notice whatsoever, even when one hit her. But the baby was squealing and grunting at the top of its voice.

"Mind where you're throwing those things!" cried Alice, wondering what on earth was going on.

"Mind your own business!" snorted the Duchess. "If everybody minded their own business, the world would go around a great deal faster than it does now."

"The world can't go faster," interrupted Alice. "It always takes twenty-four hours for the world to turn on its axis . . ."

The Duchess knew perfectly well that the axis was something at the centre of the earth on which the world spun around. But she wanted to make a joke of it.

"Talking of axes," said the Duchess to the

Cook. "Chop off the girl's head!"

Alice wasn't sure whether the Duchess was joking or not. She glanced anxiously at the Cook.

The Cook completely ignored the Duchess' words and continued stirring the soup, pretending she hadn't been listening.

"Stupid woman!" said the Duchess, before turning to Alice. "Right, girl, you can stop bothering me right now. And stop trying to show how clever you are."

And with that, the Duchess began nursing the squealing bundle in her arms. She also started singing a strange lullaby:

"Speak roughly to your little boy,
And beat him when he sneezes.
He only does it to annoy,
Because he knows it teases."

At the end of each line, the Duchess shook the baby.

Then she sang the second verse, tossing the baby violently up and down:

"I speak severely to my boy,
I beat him when he sneezes;
For he can thoroughly enjoy,
The pepper when he pleases."

As she finished the song, the Frog Footman walked in. He scowled at Alice and handed the Duchess the letter that the Fish Footman had brought. Then he left.

The Duchess took a quick glance at the invitation and got out of her chair.

"An invitation! I've got to get ready to play croquet with the Queen," she said, throwing the baby into the air, in Alice's direction. "Here, you can nurse it for a while."

Alice caught the flying bundle just before it hit the ground. The Duchess disappeared from the room without another word, but the Cook threw a frying pan after her. It just missed the Duchess' head.

The baby snorted, wriggled and squealed, trying to escape Alice's arms. But eventually it settled down and even stopped sneezing. Alice didn't know what to do now. Her first thought was to take the baby away with her. The poor thing hardly had much chance of survival if it stayed with the Duchess.

The baby grunted.

"Don't grunt," said Alice softly, trying not to frighten it any more. "Grunting is not something a little child should do."

But the baby grunted again.

The baby snorted, wriggled and squealed.

Alice pulled back the edge of the shawl that was covering its head. She could just make out the baby's face in the dim light of the kitchen. It seemed to have a rather round nose and funny little eyes. Alice didn't like the look of it at all. It looked more like a little piglet than a baby.

She said goodbye to the Cook and left the kitchen with the baby.

"Now what am I going to do with this child when I get home?" she wondered, as she walked by the forest.

Just then the baby grunted even louder, and Alice glanced down at it.

"Oh!" she screamed.

There was no mistaking it; the little creature in her arms really was a piglet.

Alice dropped the bundle in shock and the piglet scurried away.

"If it had grown up it would have made an ugly child," she said to herself. "Yet, it would have made a rather handsome pig."

Chapter 15
The Cheshire Cat

Alice was still thinking about the piglet when she saw the Cheshire Cat again. It was sitting on the bough of a tree.

The Cat grinned when it saw Alice. She thought it looked quite a good-tempered cat. Yet she saw its sharp claws and decided to speak to it in a very gentle way.

"Cheshire Puss," she said rather timidly, as she did not know its name.

The Cat's grin grew a little wider, and this encouraged Alice to continue. "Would you tell me please which way I ought to go from here?"

"That depends a good deal on where you want to get to," answered the Cat.

"I don't much care," said Alice.

"Then," purred the Cat, "it doesn't really matter which way you go."

"Not really, I suppose," said Alice, "so long as I get somewhere."

"Oh, you're sure to do that," said the Cat, "if you only walk for long enough."

Alice thought that they had exhausted the subject of which way to go. So she asked the Cat which other people or creatures lived in this part of the country.

"Well, in that direction," said the Cat, pointing its left paw to the right, "lives the Hatter." Then, pointing its right paw to the left, it said, "That's where the March Hare lives."

The Cat grinned at Alice again. "You can go and visit either of them if you like, but they are both mad."

"Oh, I don't want to go among mad people," remarked Alice.

"You can't help that," said the Cat. "Everyone here is a little mad, or strange. I'm strange. And you are certainly very strange."

"How do you know I'm strange?" asked Alice.

"You must be, or you wouldn't have come here."

Alice didn't think that proved she was strange. "And how do you know that you're strange?" she asked.

"A dog growls when it is angry and wags its tail when it's pleased," grinned the Cat. "Yet I,

The Cheshire Cat

a Cheshire Cat, do the opposite. I growl when I'm pleased and wag my tail when I'm angry. Therefore, I am strange. Anyway – enough of this madness. Tell me, are you playing croquet with the Queen today?"

"I should like to very much," said Alice, "but I haven't had an invitation."

There was no reply. The Cat had suddenly disappeared.

Alice was not surprised at this, as she was getting used to strange things happening. She began to walk on, and the next moment, the Cat reappeared as suddenly as it had disappeared.

"Have you decided where you're going?" it asked.

"I don't think so," replied Alice.

Before the last word was out, the Cat had disappeared again. Alice looked around her. Where could it have gone?

"I'll be at the croquet game," said the Cat, reappearing again. "I might see you there, if you do come."

"Why do you keep disappearing?" asked Alice.

"Do I?" said the Cat.

This time Alice kept her eyes locked on

"In that direction lives the Hatter."

the Cat. If it was going to disappear again, she would see how it did it.

And the Cheshire Cat did vanish again but very slowly indeed. Alice saw the tail disappear first. Then its legs and middle faded into nothing. Finally its head slipped away from view, leaving its grin, which remained for some time after the rest of it had gone.

"Well," said Alice, very puzzled. "I've seen a cat without a grin, but a grin without a cat! It's the most curious thing I've seen in my life."

Alice wandered on in the direction of the March Hare's house. "The Hare will be much more interesting to visit than the Hatter," she decided. "Besides, it's now the month of May. So surely the Hare can't be as mad as it was in March."

Soon after, Alice reached a small house on the edge of the wood. She thought it must belong to the Hare because the chimneys were shaped like a hare's ears, and the roof was covered with brown hare fur.

It was a large house and Alice dare not go a step further until she had nibbled another tiny piece of the mushroom to grow a little bigger. That nibble made her grow to just under two feet tall.

But for some reason she was still nervous about knocking on the door. Perhaps she was worried in case she had muddled up the months. Perhaps it really was March instead of May. If it was, then the creature might truly be mad.

At that moment she wished she had gone to visit the Hatter instead.

Chapter 16
A Strange Tea Party

In the end, Alice didn't have to knock on the March Hare's door.

The Hare was sitting outside at a table in its garden. It was having a tea party with a strange-looking fellow, who was wearing a huge top hat. Alice guessed he must be the Hatter that the Cheshire Cat had spoken of. Between them sat a Dormouse. It was fast asleep with its chin on the table.

The Hare and the Hatter were using the Dormouse as a cushion, resting their elbows on its head. "How uncomfortable for the Dormouse," thought Alice, "but I suppose it doesn't mind, as it's asleep."

The table was huge, but, strangely, the Hare, the Hatter and the Dormouse were all squeezed together at one corner of it.

"No room! No room!" they cried when they saw Alice coming.

"There's plenty of room!" said Alice

The table was huge.

indignantly, and she walked all the way down to the end of the table where the three were sitting. Then she pulled up a large armchair and sat down beside them.

"Have some wine," said the Hare in an encouraging tone.

Alice looked around the table. There was no wine in sight. There was nothing but tea. "I don't see any wine," she said.

"There isn't any," said the March Hare. "There's only tea."

"Then it wasn't very nice of you to offer it," snapped Alice.

"It wasn't very nice of you to sit down without being invited," replied the March Hare.

"I didn't know it was your table," said Alice.

The Hatter had been looking at Alice for some time with great curiosity.

"Your hair wants cutting," he said suddenly.

"It's rude to make personal remarks," answered Alice. "Very rude indeed!"

The Hatter lost interest in the discussion and poured a little hot tea on the Dormouse's nose.

"Ouch!" cried the Dormouse, waking up very suddenly.

The Hatter smiled and turned back to Alice.

"Ouch!"

"I'll give you a riddle to solve," he said. "Why is a raven like a writing desk?"

Alice didn't know the answer and asked the Hatter to tell her.

"I haven't the slightest idea," said the Hatter.

"Nor I," said the March Hare.

Alice couldn't believe it. The Hatter had asked her a riddle to which there was no answer. "Why waste time asking riddles that have no answer?" she said, angrily.

"If you knew Time as well as I do," answered the Hatter, "you wouldn't talk about wasting it."

Alice said she didn't know what the Hatter meant.

"Of course you don't!" said the Hatter, tossing his head irritably. "That's because I don't suppose you've even talked to Time!"

"Perhaps not," answered Alice cautiously. "But I know I have to beat time when I am learning to play the piano."

"Ah, that accounts for you never have talked to Time," said the Hatter. "He doesn't like being beaten. If you had been kind to him, he'd do almost anything you liked with your clock. For instance, suppose it were nine o'clock in the morning and your school lessons were just about to begin."

Alice had always hated it when lessons just began, because it would be ages before they ended.

"Pay attention!" cried the Hatter. "Imagine it is nine o'clock and lessons are just about to begin. If you were friends with Time, you could ask him to send the clock racing around, so that your lessons were over almost before they had begun. It would be time for lunch in a twinkling!"

"That would be nice," admitted Alice, before realising something. "Only . . . if lunch came so soon after breakfast, I wouldn't be hungry."

Once more the Hatter lost interest in the conversation and started talking about a person called the Queen of Hearts.

"Who is the Queen of Hearts?" asked Alice.

"Never you mind," replied the Hatter. "You'll meet her soon enough. I sang her a song once. I'll sing it for you."

The Hatter stood up and started to sing:

"Twinkle, twinkle, little bat,
How I wonder what you're at!"

When he had finished, he asked Alice if she knew the song.

"I've heard something like it," said Alice,

"but the song I knew was about a twinkling little star, not a twinkling little bat."

"Never mind," said the Hatter, and continued with his version:

"Up above the world you fly,
Like a tea tray in the sky."

The Dormouse shook itself and began singing in its sleep. *"Twinkle, twinkle, twinkle, twinkle ..."*

The Hatter pinched the poor little creature to keep it quiet, and then told Alice what happened when he was singing the song to the Queen of Hearts.

"I had hardly finished the first verse when, suddenly, the Queen bawled out, 'Mr. Hatter you're murdering Time. Off with your head!'"

"How awfully savage," said Alice. "Why would she want to chop your head off?"

"Perhaps she didn't like the way I sang," replied the Hatter. "In any case, she always wants to chop people's heads off."

Just then the March Hare gave a great yawn. He was bored with the conversation. "I'm getting tired of all this talk. Why doesn't Alice tell us a story instead?"

The Hatter started to sing.

Alice was most alarmed. "I don't know any stories," she said.

"Then the Dormouse must tell one!" said the Hatter and March Hare together.

"But it's asleep," Alice pointed out.

"I wasn't asleep," said the Dormouse, slowly opening it eyes. "I heard every word you were saying."

"Then tell us a story," said the March Hare.

"Yes, please do!" added Alice.

"And be quick about it," said the Hatter, "or else you'll be asleep again before you've told it."

"Oh dear," said the Dormouse. "In that case I had better start right away."

And so the Dormouse began its story.

Chapter 17
A Story from the Dormouse

"Once upon a time," began the Dormouse in a great hurry, "there were three little sisters. Their names were Elsie, Lacie and Tillie, and they lived at the bottom of a well."

"What did they live on?" asked Alice, who always took a great interest in questions of eating and drinking.

"They lived on treacle," said the Dormouse, after thinking about the question for several minutes.

"They couldn't have done," said Alice. "That would have made them ill."

"So they were," answered the Dormouse. "They were very ill."

Alice asked another question. "Why did they live at the bottom of a well?"

"Well," said the Dormouse after a few more minutes had passed, "it was a treacle well."

"There's no such thing!" exclaimed Alice.

"Sh! Sh!" said the Hatter impatiently. "If

you keep interrupting you might as well finish the story for yourself."

"No, please go on," said Alice very humbly. "I won't interrupt again. I suppose there could be a treacle well somewhere."

"Of course there is," said the Dormouse indignantly. "And now I will go on. Now these three little sisters were learning to draw . . ."

Alice quite forgot her promise to stop interrupting. "What were they drawing?" she asked.

"Treacle, of course!" said the Dormouse. "They were learning to draw treacle."

Alice did not want to upset the Dormouse, but she just had to ask how the three sisters had learned to draw treacle.

"You can draw a treacle well, can't you?" answered the Hatter. "So I should think it is just as easy to draw treacle from a well, eh stupid?"

Alice did not like being called stupid. "I only asked," she said sharply, "because the Dormouse said that the three sisters lived in a well. And if they actually lived in the well, how could they draw treacle from the same well?"

"Of course they were in the well," said the Dormouse, becoming a little tired of all the questions. "They were well in."

This answer so confused Alice that she let the Dormouse go on for some time without interrupting.

"They were learning to draw," the Dormouse continued, yawning and rubbing its eyes. It was getting very sleepy. "The three sisters were learning to draw all manner of things . . . everything beginning with the letter *M*."

"Why with an *M*?" asked Alice, unable to resist asking a question.

"Why not?" said the March Hare.

The Dormouse tells a story.

Alice fell silent. And so did the Dormouse. It had closed its eyes and was sinking into a doze.

The Hatter pinched the Dormouse. It woke up with a little shriek and continued the story. "They were learning to draw the moon and mousetraps, maps and monsters, memory and muchness."

"You can't draw muchness," interrupted Alice.

"Yes you can," answered the Hatter. "Drawing muchness is very much, much of a muchness."

"That's nonsense," said Alice.

"If you think it's nonsense," said the Hatter, "just keep quiet and listen to the story!"

Alice had never been spoken to so rudely. She got up from the table in great disgust and walked off. The Dormouse fell asleep immediately and neither the Hatter nor the March Hare took the least notice of Alice leaving.

Alice did look back on a couple of occasions. She rather hoped they would call after her. The last time she saw them all, the Hatter and the March Hare were trying to stuff the Dormouse into the teapot. "How cruel," she thought.

As she walked away though the wood, Alice decided she would never go back to see the

Stuffing the Dormouse into the teapot.

Hatter and March Hare. "That was the most stupid tea party I have ever been to in my life," she said to herself.

Just then, she noticed that one of the trees she was passing had a door leading right into it. "Curiouser and curiouser," she thought. "But then, everything today has been very curious. I may as well go inside the see what I find."

Alice put her hand on the doorknob and turned it.

The door opened.

Chapter 18
The Queen of Hearts

Once more, Alice found herself in the long hall, and close to the glass table. And there on top of the table was the golden key again!

She decided to take things very carefully this time. She began by using the little golden key to unlock the door that led to the garden.

Then she took the tiniest nibble from one of the bits of mushroom. She was very careful indeed about how much she ate, because she wanted to be the exact size necessary to get into the garden.

Alice's body started to shrink until she was about a foot high. Then she was able to walk through the door and down the narrow passage, towards the garden.

At last, she emerged into the garden. It was very beautiful indeed, and filled with the most colorful flowerbeds. Sprays of cool water flowed from fountains all over the garden.

A large rose bush stood near the entrance to

the garden. The roses growing on it were white. Beside the bush, three gardeners were busily painting all the roses red.

Alice thought this a very curious thing. She was also surprised at how the gardeners looked. There bodies were all oblong and flat, with their hands and feet at the corners. They looked remarkably like playing cards!

Alice had played games with cards before and she knew that cards were printed with four different symbols, Hearts, Diamonds, Clubs and Spades. Hearts and Diamonds cards were coloured red, while Clubs and Spades were black.

She had always thought that cards were rather like four different families, with ten children. Most of the cards were numbered one to ten, but each family also had a Knave, a Queen and a King.

Alice saw that the three gardeners obviously belonged to the Spades family.

And like playing cards, each one had different numbers of Spades. One gardener was numbered Two. The second was Five and the last was Seven.

"Look out, Five!" said Two. "Don't go splashing me with red paint!"

At last, she emerged into the garden.

"I couldn't help it," answered Five in a sulky manner. "Seven jogged my elbow."

"That's right, Five!" snapped Seven. "Always blame it on someone else!"

"You'd better not complain too much, Seven," answered Five. "I heard the Queen of Hearts say only yesterday that she was going to take your head off."

"What for?" asked Seven.

"For bringing the cook tulips instead of onions."

Seven flung down his brush. "Well! Of all the unjust things!" he cried. "Fancy blaming me for that!"

Just then Seven, Five and Two spotted Alice. They were very surprised to see the little girl and bowed down to her.

"Would you tell me, please," said Alice, "why are you painting the white roses red?"

Seven and Five said nothing, but Two tried to explain. "Well, you see," he said, "the fact is that this here rose bush should have been a red one. We put a white one in by mistake."

"But why is it so important to paint it red?" asked Alice.

"If the Queen of Hearts finds out that we made a mistake and grew white roses, she

"Why are you painting the white roses red?"

would have all our heads cut off!" said Two.

At that moment, Five, who had been anxiously looking across the garden, called out, "The Queen! The Queen!"

The three gardeners instantly threw themselves flat upon their faces.

There was a sound of footsteps approaching and Alice looked around. First came ten soldiers who were carrying clubs. They were followed by ten courtiers who were covered in diamonds.

Behind them were ten children, who Alice presumed were the Queen's. They were all covered in hearts. Next came the Knave of Hearts, carrying the King's crown on a crimson velvet cushion.

Behind the Knave came the King and the Queen of Hearts.

They were all shaped like the gardeners – oblong and flat.

At the rear of the procession came a group of people who Alice thought must be the Queen's guests. Alice recognised the White Rabbit among them. He was hurrying along, talking to people here and there.

The great procession came closer and closer. Alice wasn't sure whether she should lie

The procession came closer and closer.

face-down, like the gardeners. She decided against it. So she stood and waited.

When the King and Queen reached the place where Alice stood, they stopped immediately.

"Who is this?" asked the Queen of Hearts in a severe voice.

The Knave of Hearts heard the question but had no idea how to answer Her Majesty. He just bowed and smiled.

"Idiot!" cried the Queen, tossing her head impatiently and turning to Alice. "What is your name, child?"

"My name is Alice, Your Majesty," she answered very politely.

"And who are these?" asked the Queen, pointing to the three gardeners who were still lying face-down around the rose bush. In that position, the Queen could not tell whether they were gardeners or soldiers, courtiers or even her own children.

"I think they are gardeners, but how should I know?" replied Alice, surprised at her own courage. "It's no business of mine."

The Queen turned crimson with fury at Alice's boldness. She glared at Alice for a moment and then began screaming.

"Off with her head! Off with her head!"

Chapter 19
A Very Strange Game Indeed

"Nonsense!" cried Alice. "You will not remove my head."

The Queen of Hearts was furious. How could a little girl speak so rudely to her? "If I want your head off, then off will it will come!" she shouted.

The King laid a hand upon her arm. "Consider, my dear; she is only a child!" he said.

The Queen angrily turned away from Alice and ordered the Knave of Hearts to turn over the three men lying before her. The Knave did so very carefully, with one foot.

"Get up!" said the Queen in a shrill voice.

The three gardeners instantly jumped up and began bowing to the Queen, the King, the royal children and anyone else they could see to bow to.

"Stop that!" screamed the Queen. "You are making me giddy, all that bowing." She then walked over to the rose bush. "What have you been doing here?" she asked.

"May it please Your Majesty," said Two in a very humble voice, going down on one knee as he spoke, "we were trying . . ."

"I see," said the Queen, who couldn't be bothered to wait for an answer. "Off with their heads!"

And with no more ado, the royal family and its procession moved on, leaving behind three soldiers to remove three heads from three gardeners.

The gardeners ran to Alice for protection. "Don't worry," she said. "You will not be beheaded."

While the soldiers were looking the other way, she hid the three gardeners in a large garden pot. The soldiers looked everywhere, but could not find them. Eventually they gave up searching and wandered off to rejoin the royal party. Alice followed them.

"Have the gardeners lost their heads?" shouted the Queen.

"Their heads have gone, Your Majesty," the soldiers lied.

"Good!" said the Queen. "Now we can start playing croquet."

"Off with their heads!"

She turned to Alice. "Girl! Alice! Whatever your name is! Can you play croquet?"

"A little, I think," replied Alice.

"Come on then!" roared the Queen.

Alice joined the Queen, wondering what would happen next. Suddenly, she heard a timid little voice beside her.

"It's a . . . it's a very fine day," said the voice.

Alice looked and saw that it was the White Rabbit.

"Yes, it is," replied Alice. "But where's the Duchess?"

"Hush! Hush!" said the White Rabbit in a low hurried tone. He looked anxiously over his shoulder as he spoke and then raised himself on tiptoe and put his mouth close to her ear. "The Duchess is under sentence of death," he whispered.

"What for?" asked Alice.

"She was late for the game," explained the White Rabbit.

They were interrupted by the Queen calling for the game to start.

"Get to your places now," she ordered.

People began running in all directions, bumping into each other as they tried to find where they should be. Eventually they did find their places, and the game began.

Alice had never seen such a strange game. The ground itself was covered with ridges and furrows. It wasn't flat at all, as it should have been.

Instead of croquet balls, they played with live hedgehogs that had rolled themselves up. There were no mallets to hit the balls with, either. Instead each player had a flamingo bird. A player held the bird's neck and hit the rolled-up hedgehog with the bird's head.

And soldiers bent over backwards, pretending to be the iron hoops for the rolled-up hedgehogs to pass through!

Alice found it very difficult to manage her flamingo. She could tuck the bird's body under her arm with its legs hanging down. But just as she got its neck nicely straightened out to give the hedgehog a blow with its head, the bird would twist itself round and look up into Alice's face.

The flamingo had such a puzzled expression on its face at times, that Alice could not help bursting out laughing. Even when she managed to straighten out the neck again, she found that the hedgehog had unrolled itself and was heading back to its nest.

Alice had never seen such a strange game.

Besides, there was usually a great ridge or furrow in her way, whichever direction she chose to hit the hedgehog ball. The soldiers never stayed bent backwards for long, either. They often wandered off for a rest.

Alice thought that, overall, this particular game of croquet was a very difficult one indeed. The players all played at once. No one waited for their turn. They fought for their hedgehogs and stole each other's flamingoes.

Naturally, the Queen kept losing her temper. She stamped around shouting, "Off with his head!" or, "Off with her head!" at least once every minute.

Chapter 20
Off with Her Head!

"The Queen of Hearts does seem dreadfully fond of removing people's heads," thought Alice. "The great wonder is that there's anyone left alive!" She saw the Queen moving away down the field of play, so she took the opportunity to have a rest.

It was then she suddenly felt a presence. She sensed something in the air.

It puzzled her very much. She looked around for some time and then, at last, she spotted what it was. It was the familiar grin of the disappearing Cheshire Cat.

"How are you getting on?" asked the Cat, as soon as enough mouth had appeared for it to speak.

Alice was so glad to put down her flamingo and tell the Cat all about the strange croquet game. The Cat listened intently.

"I don't think they play croquet at all fairly," complained Alice. "And they all quarrel so dreadfully, one can't hear oneself speak. And they don't seem to have any rules. At least, if there are, nobody obeys them. And you've no idea how confusing it is to play with live hedgehogs, flamingoes and soldiers. I should have hit the Queen's hedgehog by now, but it always runs away when it sees my flamingo."

"How do you like the Queen of Hearts?" asked the Cat, in a low voice.

"Not at all," replied Alice. "She's so extremely . . ."

"How are you getting on?"

125

Alice broke off because the Queen had suddenly reappeared nearby and was listening to what she was saying.

"She's so extremely . . . pretty and clever . . . and likely to win the game," said Alice, changing her tune.

The Queen smiled and passed on by, giving one rolled-up hedgehog a mighty crack with her flamingo.

"Who are you talking to?" asked the King, coming up to Alice and looking at the Cat's head with some interest.

"It's a friend of mine," said Alice. "This is the Cheshire Cat. Allow me to introduce you."

The King didn't much like the look of the Cat's head at all. "However," he said, "it may kiss my hand if it likes."

"I'd rather not!" the Cat remarked.

"Don't be so rude!" said the King. "I shall have your head removed."

The King called to the Queen. "My dear, I wish you to have this Cat's head removed."

The Queen, of course, was delighted. "Off with its head!" she cried without even turning to look around. "Send for the executioner!"

The executioner arrived soon after. But then a big argument developed between the King,

"This is the Cheshire Cat."

the Queen and the executioner. The problem was clear. How could you cut off the head of something that clearly had no body? And the disappearing Cheshire Cat was then still just a head and a smile.

The executioner's argument was that you couldn't cut off a head unless it was joined to a body.

The King's argument was that anything that had a head could be executed.

The Queen's argument was that if nobody agreed what was to be done within a minute, then she would take off the heads of everyone present, the King included.

The Cheshire Cat kept its head in the end. While the King and Queen and executioner were still arguing, it simply disappeared!

Chapter 21
Alice Meets the Duchess Again

Alice was having a rest from the croquet game when the Duchess appeared again.

"You can't imagine how glad I am to see you," said the Duchess, tucking her arm around Alice as they walked off together.

Alice had never seen the Duchess in such a friendly mood. Perhaps it was only the pepper flying around in the kitchen when they first met, that had made her so horribly irritable.

"I won't have pepper in my kitchen anymore," said the Duchess. "Soup tastes just as good without it. The only thing pepper does is make people hot-tempered. That's why I am so friendly today."

The Duchess cuddled up even closer to Alice. Poor Alice didn't like her getting so friendly. For one thing, the Duchess was very ugly and smelt of onions. Also, the Duchess was exactly the right height to rest her chin on Alice's shoulder. And it was such an uncomfortably sharp chin!

Alice didn't like to be rude. So she put up with it as well as she could. "The croquet game seems to be going rather better than it was," she said, trying to keep the conversation going.

"It is so," said the Duchess, "and the moral of that is that love makes the world go around!"

"I thought," said Alice, "that it was people minding their own business that made the world go around."

"Ah well," replied the Duchess, digging her chin into Alice's shoulder more sharply than before. "Love and minding your own business are much the same thing, really. And the moral of that is to take care of the senses and the sounds will take care of themselves."

"What nonsense the Duchess is talking," thought Alice, "and how fond she is of finding a moral or a meaning in everything."

The Duchess was quiet for a while. Then she looked at the flamingo that Alice was still carrying beneath her arm.

"Watch out it doesn't bite," warned Alice.

"Very true," observed the Duchess. "Flamingoes and hot mustard both bite. And the moral of that is birds of a feather flock together."

"Only that mustard isn't a bird," remarked Alice.

The Duchess appeared again.

"Right as usual," said the Duchess.

"Mustard is a mineral, I think," said Alice.

"Of course it is!" cried the Duchess. "There's a huge mustard mine near here. And the moral of that is that the more there is of mine, the less there is of yours."

Alice changed her mind about mustard. "It's actually a vegetable, I think," she said.

"Yes, I quite agree," said the Duchess. "And the moral of that is that you must never imagine yourself not to be otherwise than what it might appear to others what you are or might have been had you been what you appeared to otherwise be."

The Duchess gasped for breath after finishing the huge sentence. Alice hadn't understood a word of it. "I might have understood that better," she said, "if I had written it all down."

"That's nothing to what I could have said," the Duchess remarked, sounding as if she was very pleased to have confused someone.

Then her mood suddenly changed. Alice felt the Duchess's body stiffen and tremble. She looked up and saw that the Queen of Hearts was standing right in front of them. Her arms were folded and she was frowning angrily.

Such an uncomfortably sharp chin!

"A fine day, Your Majesty," said the Duchess, in a low, weak voice.

The Queen had already sentenced her to lose her head . . . and now the Duchess felt it was already beginning to wobble on her shoulders.

Chapter 22
The Griffin and the Turtle

The Queen of Hearts had not forgotten that the Duchess was due to lose her head.

But at that moment she was more interested in getting Alice back to the croquet game. "Be gone with you, Duchess!" she cried.

The Duchess didn't need persuading. She was gone in a flash.

"Now let's get on with the game!" the Queen said to Alice.

Alice was much too frightened to say a word, so she simply followed the Queen back to the croquet field.

When they got there, the Queen saw that all the other players had taken the chance to sit down and rest while she was away. "Get up! Get up you lazy lot!" she cried. "Get back on the croquet field or else you know what will happen."

For the rest of the game, the Queen was more irritable than ever. She quarrelled with everyone. Anyone who argued with her was quickly removed from the field of play. "Off with his head!" she cried. "Off with her head! Off with the flamingo's head! Off with the hedgehog's head! Off with everyone's head!"

The soldiers spent the whole time taking people off to prison to await execution. Of course, that meant the soldiers had to leave their jobs as croquet hoops.

Within half an hour there were no soldiers around at all. And all the players, except the King, Queen and Alice were under arrest, waiting to have their heads removed.

Then the Queen turned to Alice. "Have you seen that old creature, the Turtle?" she asked.

"No," replied Alice. "I haven't seen the Turtle about at all. In fact, I've never met it!"

"Then we'll find it for you," replied the Queen. "Follow me."

Just as Alice began to follow the Queen, she heard the King tell a soldier to free everyone who had been taken away, to have their heads removed.

"No one will lose their heads," the King whispered, as she walked past him. "The Queen seldom remembers whose head is whose anyway; except for the Duchess'. But

"Be gone with you, Duchess!"

the Queen has ordered her head to be removed at least a hundred times so far, and it's still on her shoulders."

A few minutes later the Queen and Alice met a Griffin – an ancient monster that had the wings and head of an eagle, and the body and tail of a lion. It was lying fast asleep in the sun.

"Get up! You lazy thing!" said the Queen, giving the beast a kick. "And take this young

The Queen and Alice met a Griffin.

lady to see the Turtle. He has a story to tell, no doubt. Now I must get back to see about some executions I have ordered."

Alice wondered what the Queen would do when she found out that the King had freed everyone.

The Queen left and the Griffin rubbed its weary eyes. Then it started to laugh.

"What are you laughing about?" asked Alice.

"The Queen!" said the Griffin. "She tells everyone they will lose their head. But no one ever does. It's all her fancy. No one has ever been executed. The Queen just sends them off to the palace dungeons and the King frees them. Then as soon as the Queen has filled the dungeons again, the King just frees them all again. Now come along with me, young lady."

Alice and the Griffin went to find the Turtle. They hadn't gone very far when they spotted it, in the distance. It was sitting alone on a rock. As they came closer, Alice saw the Turtle was crying.

"Perhaps his relatives have been turned into turtle soup," said the Griffin.

When Alice reached the Turtle, she sat down beside it. "The Queen says you will tell me your story," she said.

139

"I'll tell it if you promise not to say a word until I have finished," answered the Turtle.

Alice and the Griffin settled down to listen to the story.

"Once upon a time," he finally began, "I was a young Turtle. The rest of my family and I went to school in the sea. The Master was an old turtle. We called him Tortoise . . ."

"Why?" interrupted Alice.

"Because the Tortoise taught us, silly!" said the Turtle.

"How could you ask such a silly question?" asked the Griffin. "Now Mr. Turtle, continue your story."

The Turtle explained how they had gone to school every day.

"So did I," interrupted Alice again. "And we learned lots of special extra subjects like French and music."

"But did you learn clothes washing at your school?" asked the Griffin.

"Certainly not!" replied Alice, indignantly.

"Ah then," said the Griffin, "you can't have gone to a good school. Special subjects at our school included French, music, ambition, distraction, uglification and derision, and washing clothes."

The Turtle was crying.

"I never heard of uglification," said Alice. "What is it?"

"The opposite of beautification . . ."

Before Alice could ask any more questions, it was the Turtle's turn to tell what subjects he studied at school. "There was mystery, ancient and modern, sea-ography, beach-ology, ocean-geography, seaweed science and drawing lessons with an ancient whale, who swam in once a week to teach us."

"How many hours were you at school each day?" asked Alice.

"Ten hours the first day," answered the Turtle, "Nine hours the next, eight hours the next and so on."

"What a curious plan," said Alice.

"That's the reason they're called lessons," said the Griffin, "because they lessen by an hour each day."

That made Alice laugh – but not as much as when the Turtle and Griffin decided to teach her a special dance.

Chapter 23
Dancing with Lobsters

"You have not lived under the sea, have you?" asked the Turtle.

"No," said Alice, "I have never lived in, on, or under the sea."

"And have you," said the Turtle, "ever been introduced to a lobster?"

"I once tasted a . . ." Alice bit her tongue before she said another word. She had indeed tasted a lobster at dinner, and she had found it most delicious. But she realised it might be unwise to talk about having eaten one in front on some creatures that might well be friends with the local lobsters.

"Er, no I have never had the honour of meeting a lobster," Alice fibbed.

"So," cried the Turtle, "you can have no idea what a delightful thing a Lobster Quadrille is?"

"No idea at all," said Alice. "Do tell me what it is!"

"Well," said the Griffin, "a lobster is a lobster and lives in the sea."

"I know what a lobster is," interrupted Alice, "but not what a Quadrille is."

"Then I shall tell you in a verse," said the Turtle.

"Beneath the waters of the sea,
Are lobsters thick as thick as can be –
And they love to dance with you and me."

The Turtle finished the verse and then announced to Alice that the Quadrille was the name of a dance.

"What sort of dance?" asked Alice.

"Why," said the Griffin, "you first form into a line on the seashore."

"Lots of lines really," interrupted the Turtle. "Lines of lobsters, seals, turtles, salmon, and so on. But you make sure you've cleared all the jellyfish out of the way first."

"That generally takes some time," announced the Griffin. "But then the dance starts and you advance twice, each with a lobster as a partner."

"Of course," said the Turtle. "Advance and change partners."

"Yes, change lobsters and take two steps back," continued the Griffin.

"I know what a lobster is."

"And then," said the Turtle, becoming quite excited, "you throw the lobsters as far out to sea as you can!"

"Then you swim after them," cried the Griffin, pretending to be swimming.

"Turn a somersault in the sea," shouted the Turtle, leaping up and down.

"Change lobsters once again," yelled the Griffin at the top of its voice.

"And back to land again," finished the Turtle, almost out of breath.

Alice didn't know what to say. "It must be an exhausting dance," she said at last.

"Well, we shall do it," said the Turtle. "But of course we'll have to do it without lobsters for now."

"And the Turtle can sing," said the Griffin.

So the Turtle began to sing in verse about a fish called a whiting and some other creatures:

> "'Will you walk a little faster,' said a whiting
>   to a snail.
> 'There's a porpoise close behind, and he's
>   treading on my tail.
> See how eagerly the lobsters and the turtles
>   all advance!

The Lobster Quadrille.

They are waiting on the shingle – will you
  come and join the dance?
Will you, won't you, will you, won't you,
  will you join the dance?
Will you, won't you, will you, won't you,
  won't you join the dance?

'You really have no notion how delightful it
  will be
When they take us up and throw us, with the
  lobsters, out to sea!'
But the snail replied 'Too far, too far!' and
  gave a look askance –
Said he thanked the whiting kindly, but he
  would not join the dance
Would not, could not, would not, could not,
  would not join the dance.
Would not, could not, would not, could not,
  could not join the dance.

'What matters it how far we go?' his scaly
  friend replied,
'There is another shore, you know, upon the
  other side.
The further off from England the nearer is
  to France –
Then turn not pale, beloved snail, but come
  and join the dance.

Will you, won't you, will you, won't you,
will you join the dance?
Will you, won't you, will you, won't you
join the dance?' "

Alice watched as they finished the dance. "Thank you, it was very interesting to see," she said, feeling very glad that it was all over at last. "And I do so like that song about the whiting fish."

"Have you seen a whiting before?" asked the Turtle.

"Oh yes," said Alice. "I've often seen them on dinner plates . . ."

Once more Alice had to stop herself from speaking. What would the Turtle have thought if he knew she ate his friends!

"You say you've seen them on Dinner Plates," said the Turtle. "I don't know where that is. But if you met a whiting there, Dinner Plates must be a nice place to go to."

Chapter 24
Why a Whiting is Called a Whiting

After the dance, the Griffin began a long discussion about the whiting and all its habits. Alice was so very bored.

"My, my," she said, with a yawn. "I have never heard so much about a whiting before."

"I can tell you more," said the Griffin. "Do you know why it's called a whiting?"

"I never even thought about it," said Alice, hiding another big yawn.

"Because it cleans boots and shoes. That's why," said the Griffin.

Alice was very puzzled. "Cleans boots and shoes?"

"What do you clean your boots and shoes with?" asked the Griffin.

"Why, with a polish called blacking," replied Alice.

"Well there you are," said the Griffin. "Under the sea it's done by the whiting."

"But you don't have boots and shoes under the sea," puzzled Alice.

"Yes we do," insisted the Griffin.

"And what are they made of?" asked Alice.

"Why, mainly soles and eels, of course," said the Griffin. "Any shrimp could have told you that."

"Mind you," said the Turtle, "I wouldn't go and see a whiting unless I had a porpoise to do so."

"Don't you mean 'purpose'?" asked Alice.

"I mean what I say," said the Turtle. "No fish would go anywhere without a porpoise."

Alice giggled.

The Griffin asked if Alice knew any poems about lobsters.

Alice did know one and recited it.

"'Tis the voice of the Lobster; I heard him declare,
'You have baked me too brown, I must sugar my hair.'
As a Duck with its eyelids, so he with his nose
Trims his belt and his buttons, and turns out his toes.

*When the sands are all dry, he is as happy as
    a lark,
And will talk in ridiculous tones of the shark.
But when the tide rises and sharks are
    around,
His voice has a timid and very quiet sound."*

The Turtle thought the verse nonsense. But
the Griffin insisted Alice should recite the
second verse too.

*"I passed by his garden, and marked with
    one eye,
How the Owl and the Panther were sharing
    a pie.
The Panther took piecrust, gravy and meat,
While the Owl had the dish as its share of
    the treat.
When the pie was all finished, the Owl, as a
    boon,
Was kindly permitted to pocket the spoon."*

The Griffin said he had never heard such a
strange poem. The Turtle agreed.

The Griffin wondered what they could do
next, and suggested they might try another
Lobster Quadrille.

The Owl and the Panther.

"Oh no," said Alice. "Instead, I think the Turtle should give us a verse about turtles."

"I'm too sad to give you a poem," the Turtle replied. "Too many of my friends have been vanishing into the soup pot."

Just as the Turtle finished speaking, they all heard the voice of the White Rabbit, in the distance.

"Hear ye! Hear ye! The trial is about to begin. Take your places in the courthouse immediately!"

"Come on!" cried the Griffin, taking Alice by the hand and hurrying off.

"What trial is it?" panted Alice.

But all that the Griffin would say was, "Hurry on! Hurry on! We mustn't be late!"

Chapter 25
Who Stole the Tarts?

The Griffin and Alice rushed into the court-house, and found the King and Queen of Hearts already seated on their throne. Alice wondered what on earth was going on. There seemed to be some sort of trial. But who was on trial?

A huge crowd had gathered to witness whatever was about to start. There were funny human beings, little birds and beasts, a lobster or two, the Parrot and the Dodo, not quite as dead as most dodos are. Bill the Lizard was there, and so were the Frog and Fish Footmen. Alice also spotted some guinea-pigs, the Hatter, a flamingo or three, hedgehogs, a newt, rabbits, mice, dogs, fish and the Duchess.

Oh! And high on a ledge above the throne was the Cheshire Cat, smiling and then disappearing and reappearing to its heart's content.

In the middle of the court was a table with a large dish of jam tarts on it. They looked so

Who was on trial?

good that it made Alice quite hungry. "I wish they would get on with whatever they want to do," she said. "The sooner they start, the sooner they finish, and the quicker I'll be able to eat one of those tarts."

Just then, the White Rabbit entered the court with a big scroll under its left arm, and a trumpet in its right hand.

Alice had not been in a courtroom before, but she had read about them. She could see that the King was to be the judge, because he was wearing a great big wig. Then she saw the Knave of Hearts. He was standing and facing the King. She guessed that it was the Knave of Hearts who was to stand trial.

Beside the throne were twelve chairs inside a wooden enclosure.

"That must be the jury-box," Alice whispered to the Griffin.

Each chair inside the jury-box was occupied by a bird or another creature. They were the jury who would listen to the evidence and decide if the Knave of Hearts was guilty. Each one had a stick of chalk and a small slate to write on.

Alice saw that they were already writing something down.

"What are they doing?" she asked the Griffin. "They can't have anything to write down yet, because the trial has not begun."

"They are putting down their names," answered the Griffin, "just in case they forget them by the end of the trial."

"Stupid creatures!" cried out Alice, quite loudly.

"Silence in court!" boomed the White Rabbit. Even the King put on his spectacles and peered around the court, trying to see who had dared to speak.

One of the jurors, a penguin, had some chalk that squeaked. This really annoyed Alice. So she went around to the back of the jury-box and snatched the chalk. She did it so quickly that the penguin didn't notice it was gone until later. It spent the rest of the trial trying to write with a claw.

"White Rabbit! Read the charges!" called out the King.

The White Rabbit blew three noisy blasts on the trumpet. Then it unrolled the parchment and began to read it:

"The Queen of Hearts, she made some tarts,
All on a summer day.

The jury would listen to the evidence.

The Knave of Hearts, he stole those tarts,
And took them quite away."

"Members of the jury," said the King, "consider your verdict. Is the Knave of Hearts innocent or guilty of stealing the tarts?"

"Not yet! Not yet!" cried the White Rabbit. "You have to hear the evidence first."

"Call the first witness!" cried the King.

The White Rabbit blew three more blasts on the trumpet and called out, "First witness!"

The first witness was the Hatter. He came in with a teacup in one hand and a piece of bread and butter in the other. "I beg your pardon, Your Majesty, for bringing these in," he said, "but I hadn't quite finished my tea when I was sent for."

"You ought to have finished," said the King sternly. "When did you start your tea?"

The Hatter looked at the March Hare, who had followed him into court, arm-in-arm with the Dormouse. "The fourteenth of March, I think," answered the Hatter.

"Fifteenth!" cried the March Hare.

"Sixteenth!" squeaked the Dormouse.

"Write that down," the King said to the jury, and the jury eagerly wrote down all three dates

Blowing three noisy blasts on the trumpet.

on their slates. After doing that, they added them all up, subtracted a half and added three quarters.

The Hatter was completely confused now; so confused that he took a bite out of his teacup and swallowed a sip of bread and butter.

That was the moment Alice felt a curious sensation. "Oh my goodness," she thought, "I'm starting to grow again!"

Chapter 26
Alice Grows Again

"I wish you wouldn't squeeze me so much," said the Dormouse, who was now sitting beside Alice in the court.

"I can't help it," replied Alice. "I'm starting to grow!"

"You've no right to grow here," said the Dormouse.

"Nonsense!" said Alice. "You're growing too."

"Yes," said the Dormouse, "but I grow at a sensible pace – not like you."

With that, the Dormouse scuttled off to find another seat in the court.

Meanwhile, the Hatter was still trying to remember what evidence he could give the court. But all he could think of was how late he had started his tea that day, and how the bread was rather thin.

The King was running out of patience. "Give your evidence now," he boomed, "or else the Queen will have your head!"

"I will give you my evidence," said the Hatter, "in a twinkling of a . . ."

"The twinkling of a what?" asked the King.

"It began with the tea," the Hatter replied.

"Of course, the word twinkling begins with a T!" said the King sharply. "Don't take me for a dunce! Go on with your evidence."

"I will," said the Hatter. "I remember now. The March Hare said . . ."

"I didn't!" cried the March Hare, before

"I'm starting to grow!"

the Hatter even had time to say what he wanted to say.

"Yes, you did!" cried the Hatter.

"I deny it!" said the March Hare.

"He denies it," said the King.

"Anyway," said the Hatter, "the Dormouse said . . ."

The Hatter looked around expecting the Dormouse to deny it too. But the Dormouse denied nothing because he was now fast asleep.

"After that," continued the Hatter, who seemed to be talking complete and utter nonsense, "I cut some more bread and butter . . ."

Again the Hatter was interrupted. "But what did the Dormouse say?" asked a member of the jury.

"That I can't remember now," answered the Hatter.

"You must remember," said the King.

The miserable Hatter dropped his teacup and bread and butter, and went down on one knee. "Your Majesty," he said, "I have a very poor memory."

"You're certainly a very poor speaker," said the King.

At that point, one of the guinea-pigs began cheering.

"Silence that creature!" the King cried angrily.

A court official grabbed the guinea-pig, put it into a large canvas bag and tied up the top with string. Just for good measure, he then sat on it.

For some strange reason all the other guinea-pigs started cheering. They were all put in bags and thrown out of court.

"That finishes with the guinea-pigs," said Alice. "At least we can get on now." She was beginning to think that the trial might never end.

The King asked the Hatter if he had anything else to say.

"No," said the Hatter, "except that I'd like to finish my tea."

"You may go," said the King at last.

The Hatter hurried out of court. As he left the court, the Queen called out, "Off with his head!"

The next witness was the Duchess' cook. She came into court carrying a big box of pepper. All the people and creatures by the door began to sneeze.

"Give your evidence, Cook," boomed the King. "Tell me, what were the tarts made of?"

"I have a very poor memory."

"Pepper, mostly," said the Cook.

"And treacle," said the sleepy voice of the Dormouse.

"Silence!" sneezed the Queen. "Turn that Dormouse out of court. Pinch him! Off with his head and his whiskers too!"

For some minutes the whole of the court was in confusion as the officials tried to get the Dormouse out. By the time it had been done, the Cook has vanished.

"Never mind," said the King, clearly happy that another witness had been finished with. Then he turned to the Queen. "My dear, this is all so tiring. My head is aching. You must speak to the next witness."

The White Rabbit gave three blasts on the trumpet and announced the next witness.

To Alice's surprise, she heard her own name called out!

Chapter 27
Alice's Evidence

Alice got up from her seat, quite forgetting how much she had grown. She hit her head on the ceiling and her dress caught on the edge of the jury-box. All the jury tumbled out, falling on the heads of the people below.

"Oh, I *beg* your pardon!" she exclaimed, picking up each one and putting them back in the box.

"The trial cannot continue," said the King, in a very serious voice, "until all the jurymen and creatures are put back in their box properly."

The King was staring at Alice as he spoke. She looked down and saw that in her hurry, she had put the little penguin back into the box upside down. The poor creature was waving its feet in the air, in alarm.

Alice turned the penguin the right way up again. "Though I doubt it would be of much use to the trial, whichever way up it was," she thought.

Finally she entered the witness box.

"What do you know about this matter?" asked the King.

"Nothing," said Alice.

"Nothing whatever?" replied the King.

"Nothing whatever," insisted Alice.

"Now that's very important," said the King, turning to the jury.

They had just started to write down the word "important" in their notes, when the White Rabbit interrupted. "Surely you mean unimportant, Your Majesty?"

"Do I? Oh yes. Of course I do." said the King. "Members of the jury, you will write that down immediately."

The King fell silent for a moment and then suddenly made an announcement: "All persons more than a mile high must leave the court!"

Everyone looked at Alice.

"I'm not a mile high," said Alice.

"Yes you are!" said the King.

"Nearly two miles high, I should think," said the Queen.

"Well," said Alice, obstinately, "I shall not go. You just invented that rule."

"It's the oldest rule in Wonderland," said the King.

"Oh, I beg your pardon!"

It was the first time that Alice had heard someone call this strange land by name. "At least," she thought, "I know where I am now, even if I still haven't any idea where Wonderland is."

The King interrupted her thoughts. "You may sit down," he said. "I have decided I don't wish to hear any more evidence."

All at once, the White Rabbit jumped up in a great hurry and gave yet another loud blast on the trumpet. "Your Majesty," it said, "I have one more piece of evidence. I have this envelope."

"What's in it?" asked the Queen.

"I don't know," said the White Rabbit. "I haven't opened it yet."

"Open it immediately," said the King.

The White Rabbit opened the envelope and announced that there was nothing inside.

"Very important evidence indeed," said the King. "Probably the most important piece of evidence yet. It surely proves that the Knave of Hearts stole the tarts."

Alice shook her head in disbelief. How could an empty envelope prove anything?

"At last we can finish the trial," sighed the Queen. And with that, she flung an inkpot

Everyone looked at Alice.

at poor little Bill the Lizard, who was also a member of the jury.

The King told the jury to give their final verdict.

"No!" said the Queen. "First, the Knave of Hearts must be told what his punishment is and then whether he is innocent or guilty."

"Stuff and nonsense!" cried Alice. "You can't punish someone before the jury has decided whether he is guilty or innocent."

"Hold your tongue!" cried the Queen, turning purple with anger.

"I won't!" shouted Alice.

"Off with her head!" shouted the Queen at the top of her voice. "Off with her head . . . off with her head . . . off with her head . . . off with her head!"

The Queen's guards rushed towards Alice, but Alice didn't care.

"You can't take off my head," she heard herself say. "You are not a real Queen. Nor is the King a King. You are all just playing cards! All of you!"

And as soon as those words left her lips, the King, Queen and guards all did turn into real playing cards. Alice saw them flying up into the air, fluttering all over the place. She put her hands above her head to protect herself from all the cards tumbling down and gave a little scream . . .

Chapter 28
A Dream of Wonderland?

The next moment Alice found herself back in the meadow, where she had been having the picnic with her sister. She opened her eyes and saw some leaves fluttering down from the tree above her. Then she saw her sister, sitting close by.

"Wake up! Wake up, Alice dear!" said her sister. "What a long sleep you've had!"

Alice sat up and looked around. She was very confused for a while. "I've had the most curious dream," she said.

Alice told her sister everything she could remember about the dream. When she had finished, her sister laughed.

"That certainly was a curious dream," she said.

"Yes, it was very strange indeed," answered Alice, sleepily watching the setting sun. As she watched, she almost dozed off again. Her eyes closed and as they did, the whole meadow seemed to come alive with the strange creatures of her dream.

The long grass rustled at her feet as the White Rabbit hurried by, and the frightened Mouse splashed through the pond.

She heard the rattle and ringing of the teacups as the March Hare, the Hatter and the Dormouse had their tea party. She also heard the shriek of the Griffin, the sobbing of the Turtle and the shrill voice of the Queen crying, "Where's Alice? Off with her head!"

"What a long sleep you've had!"

She saw the baby pig sneezing on the Duchess' knees and Bill the Lizard flying out of the chimney, too.

Alice believed herself to be back in Wonderland. She wondered what would happen if she opened her eyes again. Would everything change back to the real world?

When Alice finally did open her eyes, the grass was rustling in the wind, but there was no White Rabbit to be seen. The wind was making ripples on the pond, but there was no sign of the Mouse.

The bells hanging around the necks of the cows in the field were ringing but there were no tinkling teacups of the Hatter's tea party. All she saw was a lone hare running alongside the hedge.

Alice heard a piglet squealing, but she could not see the Duchess or her strange baby.

All sorts of noises were coming from the nearby farmyard and for a moment, Alice wondered if she could hear the shriek of the Griffin and the sobs of the Turtle.

She looked across the meadow and up to the chimney on her home. There was no smoke – and no Bill the Lizard shooting out of the top of it.

Alice almost dozed off again.

Alice also stared up into the branches of the tree above her. There was not a hint of a grin from a Cheshire Cat, nor a sign of the Queen of Hearts crying, "Off with her head!"

Yet, Alice was sure that Wonderland had been real. No one would ever convince her otherwise. Perhaps some day she would tell the story to her own children.

It would remind her forever of a picnic with her sister, a most curious dream, and a happy childhood day in a sunny meadow, long ago.

The End